For Hilary – who made all the right noises

THE NOISY BABY
by Moira Kemp

British Library Cataloguing in Publication Data
A catalogue record of this book is available from
the British Library.
ISBN 0 340 79944 7 (PB)

The right of Moira Kemp to be identified
as the author and illustrator of this Work has
been asserted by her in accordance with
the Copyright, Designs and Patents Act 1988.

First edition published 2003
10 9 8 7 6 5 4 3

Published by Hodder Children's Books
a division of Hodder Headline Limited
338 Euston Road London NW1 3BH

Printed in China

The Noisy Baby

MOIRA KEMP

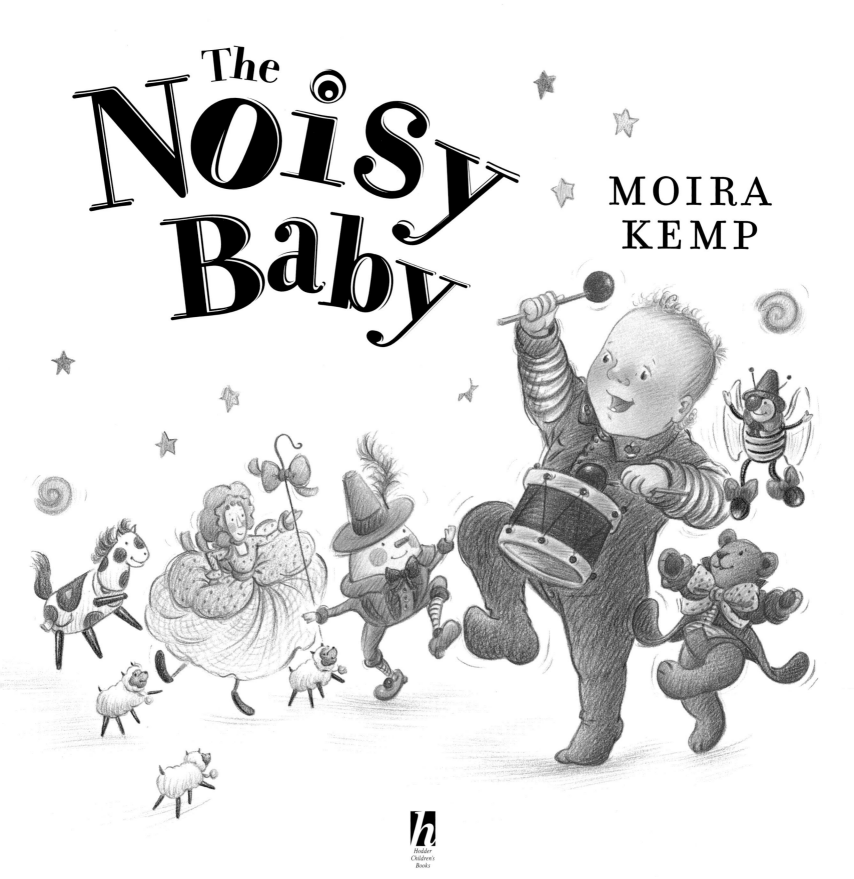

h
Hodder
Children's
Books

A division of Hodder Headline Limited

Once upon a time there was a royal baby
who loved to bang on his little red drum.

He banged on his little red drum all day long.
And all night too.

And this is the noise he made . . .

. . . until his mother picked him up and said,
'I think it's time to play *hush-a-bye-baby*.'
And she bundled him off to his grandpa, the king.

'Now be a good boy
for Grandpa,' she said.
Then she tucked the
little red drum under
her arm and off
she went.

The king played *peepo*. The baby frowned.

The king played *fingers-and-toes*.
The baby sniffed.

The king played *bumpety-bumpety-bump* and the baby opened his mouth and this is the noise he made . . .

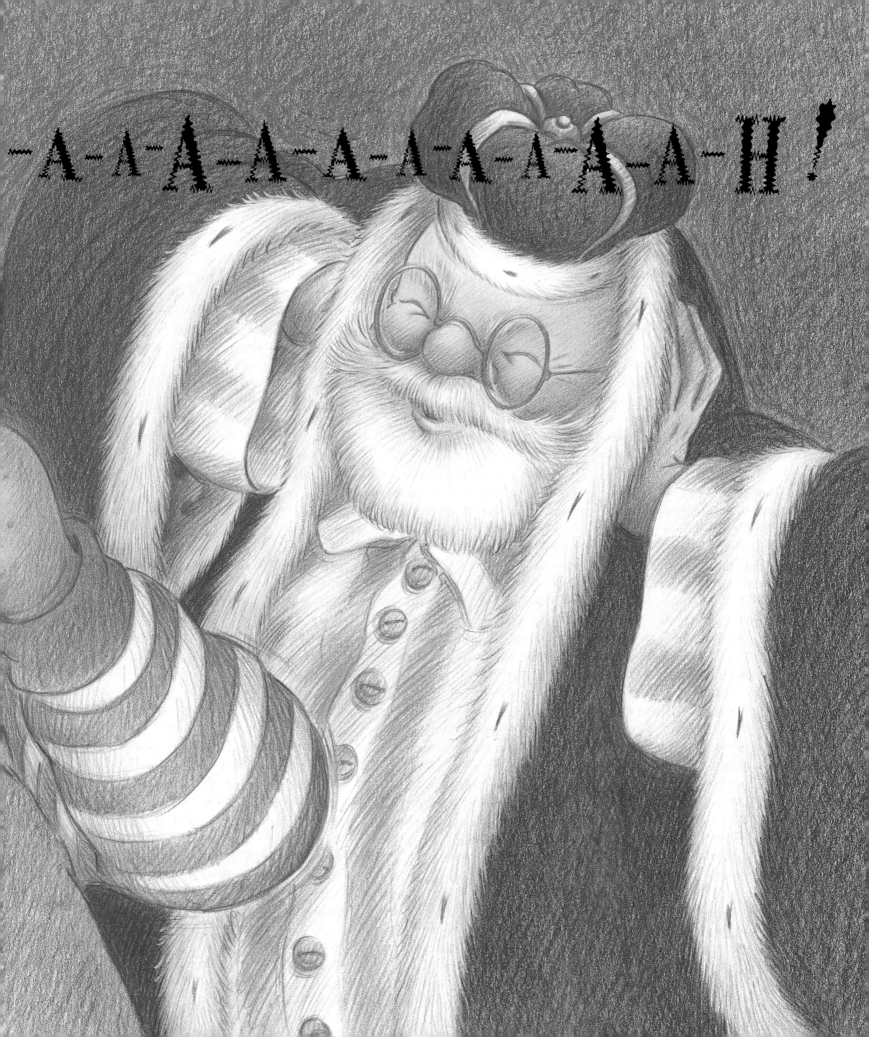

So the king played *wibbling and wobbling* . . .

and *teetering* . . .

and *tottering* . . .

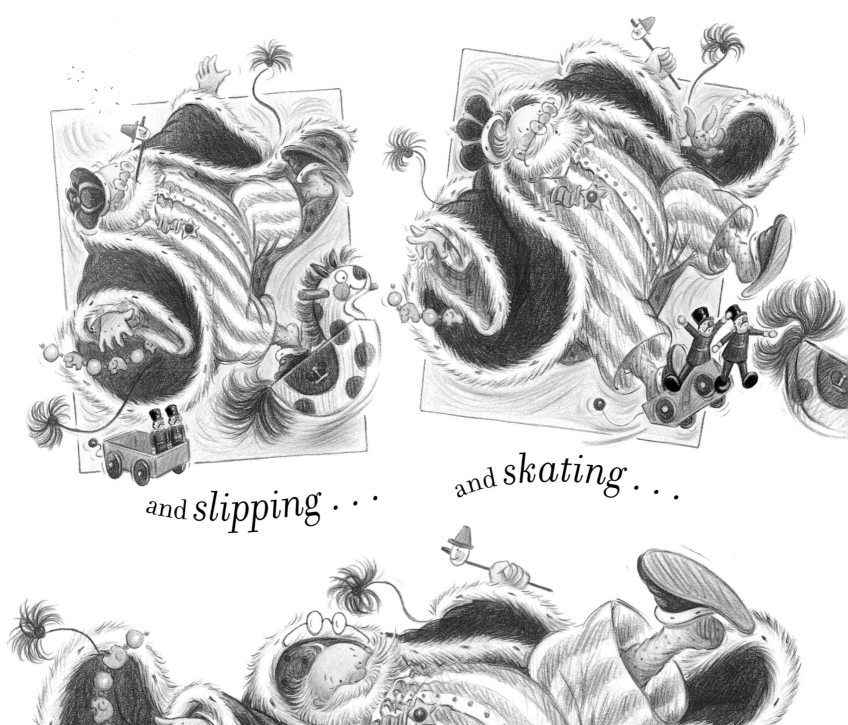

and *slipping* . . .

and *skating* . . .

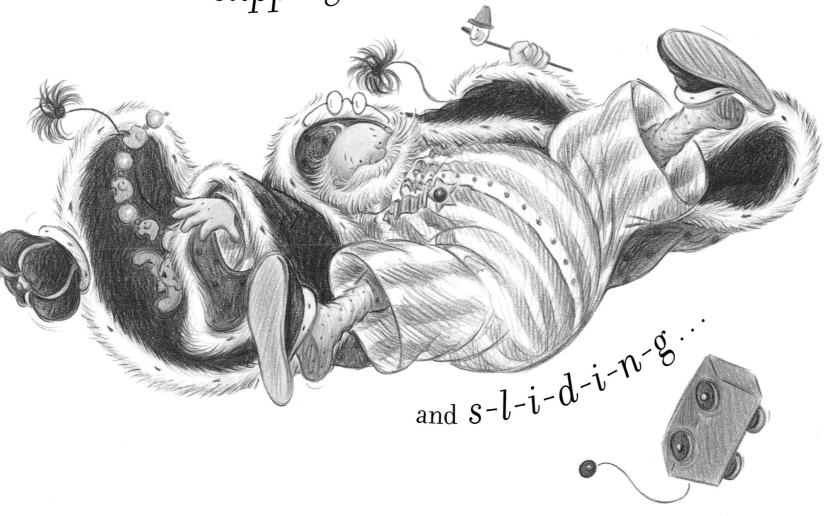

and s-l-i-d-i-n-g . . .

And then  banging and bashing and crashing!

The baby looked
at the king and
stopped crying.

The baby looked
at the king and
started giggling.

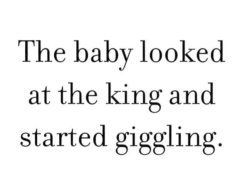

The baby looked at
the king and he
opened his mouth
and this is the
noise he made . . .

hee hee hee hee hee hee hee hee hee hee hee
hee hee hee hee hee hee hee hee hee hee hee
hee hee hee hee hee hee hee hee
hee hee hee hee hee hee hee hee hee hee hee hee hee
hee hee hee hee hee hee hee hee hee hee hee hee
hee hee hee hee hee hee hee hee

. . . until the king picked him up and said,

'I think it's time to play raising-a-royal-racket.'

And he swung the baby onto his shoulders and off they went romping and stomping through the palace.

They whooped and they whistled.
They **howled** and they **hooted**.
They shrieked and they shouted.

Then they all opened their mouths together and this is the noise they made . . .

. . . until the princess opened her door and said,

'Who's making this terrible racket?'

The baby looked at his mother and frowned.

The baby looked at his mother and sniffed.

The baby looked at his mother and his mother opened her arms and said, 'I think it's time to play *rock-a-bye-baby.*'

Then she hugged
him and the baby
yawned.

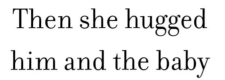

She cuddled
him and
snuggled him
and the
baby closed
his eyes.

She rocked him gently to and fro and the baby
opened his mouth and this is the noise he made . . .

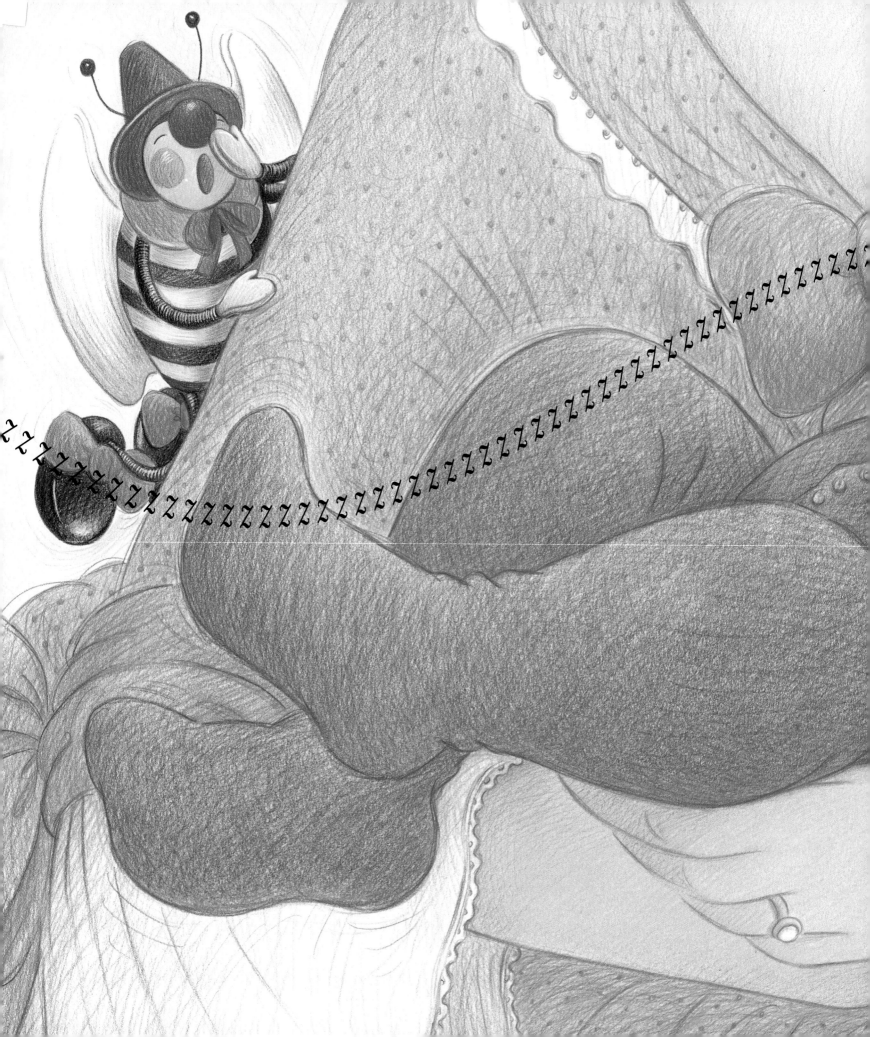